Night on the Sand

Monica Mayper   Art by Jaime Kim

CLARION BOOKS
An Imprint of HarperCollinsPublishers
Boston   New York

Clarion Books is an imprint of HarperCollins Publishers.

Night on the Sand
Text copyright © 2022 by Monica Mayper
Illustrations copyright © 2022 by Jimyung Kim

clarionbooks.com

Library of Congress Cataloging-in-Publication Data is available.
ISBN: 978-1-328-88418-3

The illustrations in this book were done in watercolor
with digital techniques.
The text was set in Stone ITC Std.
Interior design by Mary Claire Cruz and Kaitlin Yang

Manufactured in Italy
RTLO 10 9 8 7 6 5 4 3 2 1

First Edition

For Martha: true compass —M. M.

For my dad —J. K.

There was a howl,
a dark whirl of wind and power.

Roof from wall,

stone from stone,

first our house, then silence fell.

It was night, and cold.

We could not find our father, mother.

Only each other.

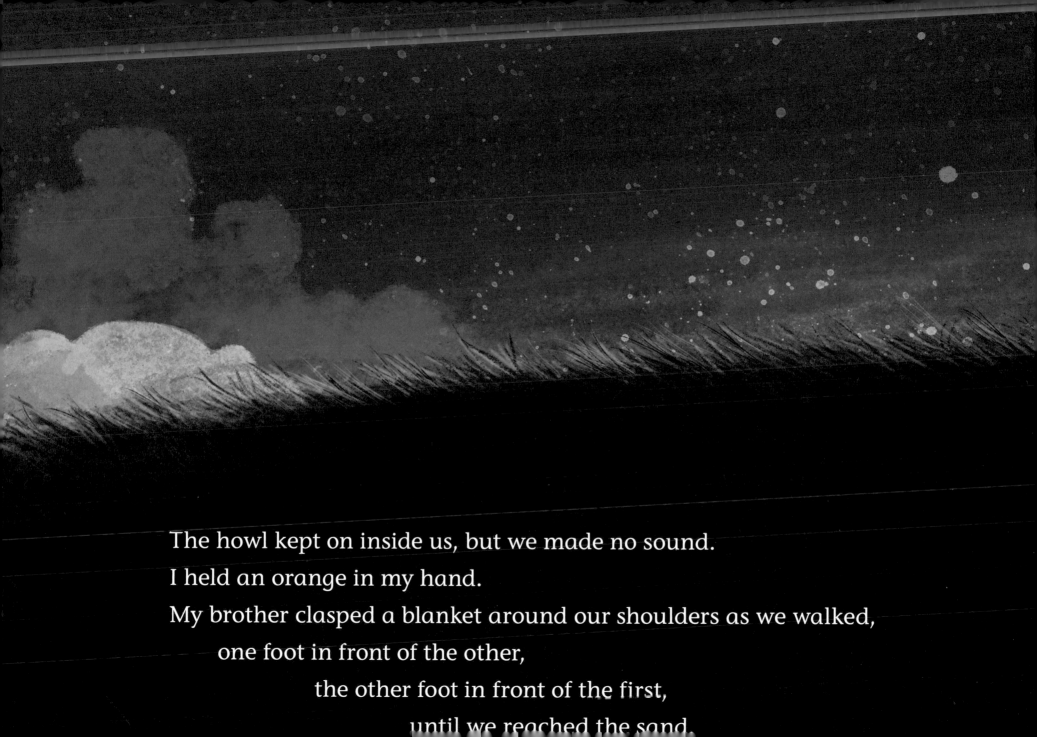

The howl kept on inside us, but we made no sound.

I held an orange in my hand.

My brother clasped a blanket around our shoulders as we walked,

one foot in front of the other,

the other foot in front of the first,

until we reached the sand.

We lay down on the beach to sleep.

I cradled my orange close.

My brother kept the blanket over us.

The moon and stars looked down.
We were not alone.

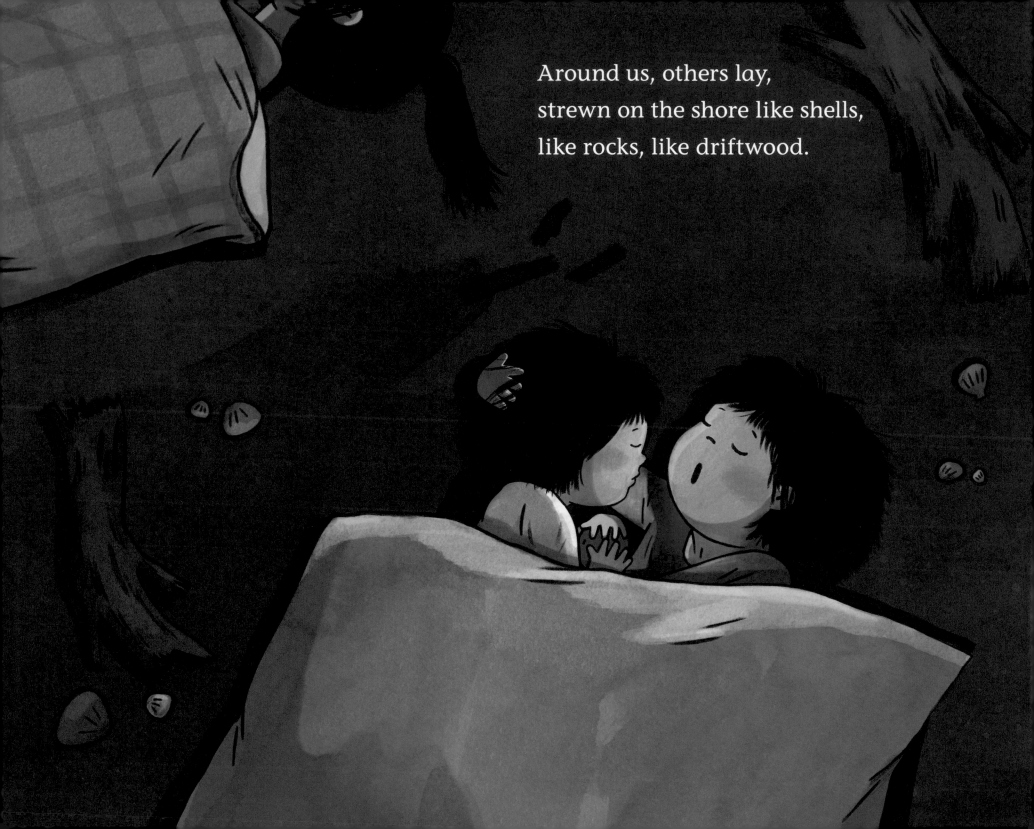

Around us, others lay,
strewn on the shore like shells,
like rocks, like driftwood.

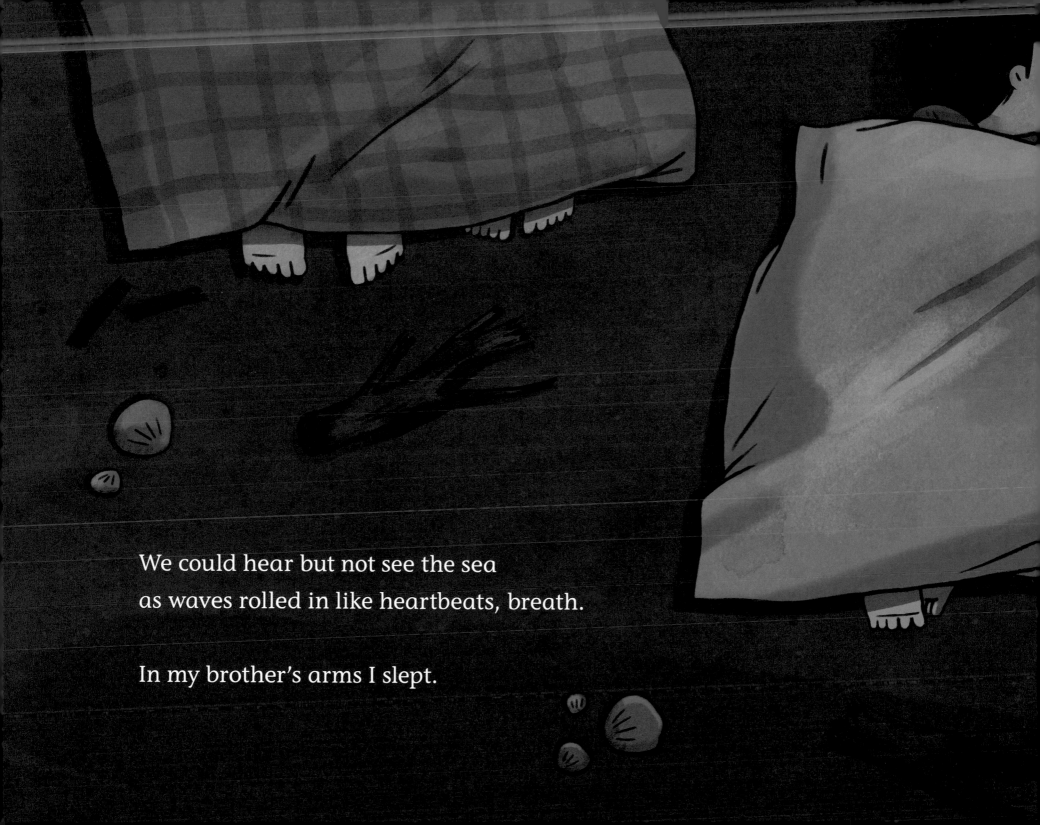

We could hear but not see the sea
as waves rolled in like heartbeats, breath.

In my brother's arms I slept.

Morning came.
Above, sea birds cried, *Pío, pío.*

Inside me too was a raw cry. I could not let it out.

I still clutched my orange in my hands.

My brother kept his arm around me. His eyes looked far away.

My stomach gnawed and growled.

"Hungry?" whispered my brother.

"Yes," I whispered back.

Those were our first words.

We were not alone.

A boy had caught three small fish in his net.

A woman and a girl gathered wood.

A man pulled some bread from his bag.

Another offered water from his flask.

The fire was warm and smoked as we gathered close.

The sun slowly warmed us too. The wind stayed low.

The waves gently brushed the shore.

Booom shhhhh Booom shhhhh Booom shhhhh

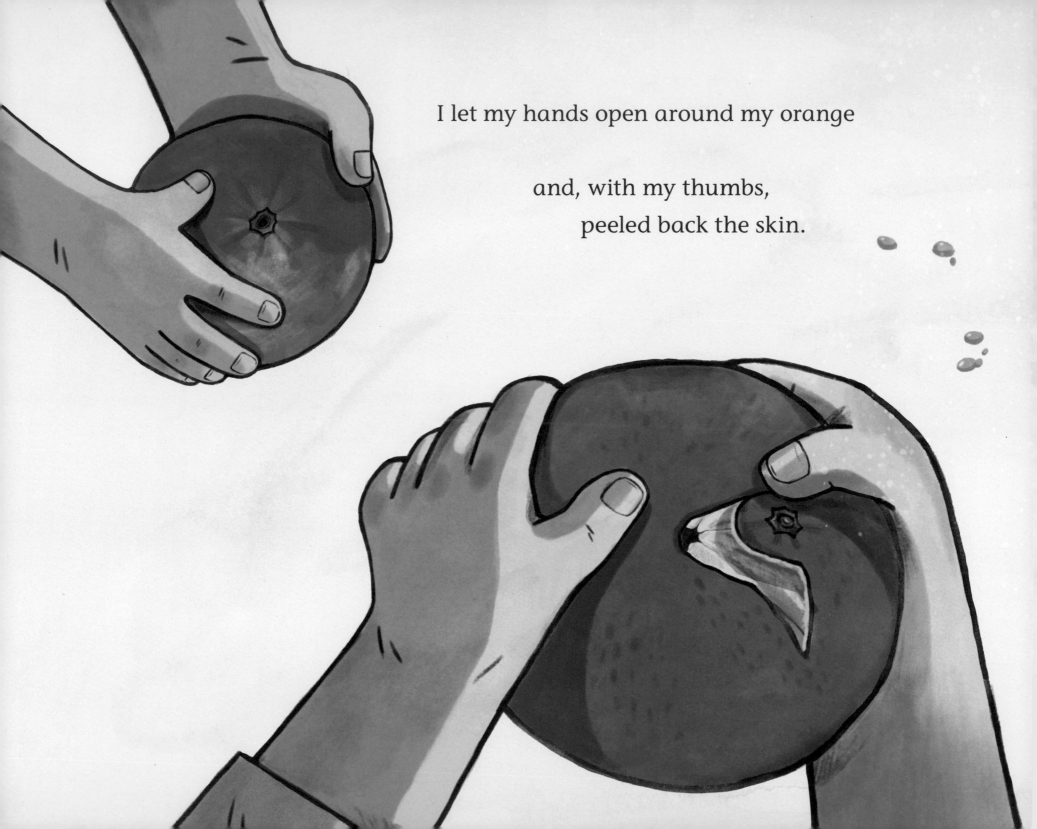

I let my hands open around my orange

and, with my thumbs,
peeled back the skin.

It smelled like a garden flower—sweet,

with the smoke and salt and fish and sea.

I broke it into pieces, and gave the first one to my brother.

I ate one, then shared the rest to reaching hands.

I could hear my own heartbeat, breath move with the
booom shhhh of the waves.

"Look, a boat," my brother said. "For us."

We scrambled to our sandy feet, clasped hands.

We helped each other in.

We could not go back.

Only on, to the new we did not know
that waited on the other shore.

We were not alone.

Author's Note

Near and far, as of this writing, at least 80 million people on our shared planet can be counted as refugees, forcibly displaced or uprooted from their homes and their lives by natural disaster and by human conflict. Fueled by climate change, this number—more than half of them children—will almost certainly grow as our century advances.

Those who have lived through such experiences share their own stories with grace, insight, and the power of authenticity. *Night on the Sand* does not try to recount events that happened to specific people at a particular time, focusing instead on our human connection, our capacity even at the darkest moment to join hands and set one foot in front of the other. The brothers' experience of catastrophe is harrowing, but they do not travel alone.

You may find that pieces of the brothers' story connect with your own. In every journey, there are places and people we leave behind or who leave us. There are those we walk alongside on a brief stretch of sand. And there are those as yet unknown who may choose to reach out when we are in need, to help us onto a new shore. We in turn may be called to play each or all of these roles in the lives of others.

To learn more about refugees and displaced persons, as well as how you can help, please visit the International Rescue Committee (IRC) at rescue.org or the United Nations Refugee Agency (UNHCR) at unhcr.org.